dauid orme

has written too many books to count, ranging from poetry to non-fiction.

When he is not writing he travels around the UK, giving performances and running writing workshops.

David is a huge science fiction fan and has the biggest collection of science fiction magazines that the Starchasers have ever seen.

starchasers

the planet of the vampires

by

dauid orme

illustrated by
jorge mongiovi

starchasers

The Planet of the Vampires
by David Orme

Illustrated by Jorge Mongiovi

Published by Ransom Publishing Ltd.
51 Southgate Street, Winchester, Hants. SO23 9EH, UK

www.ransom.co.uk

ISBN   978 184167 765 1

First published in 2009

A CIP catalogue record of this book is available from the British Library.

misha hanson

captain

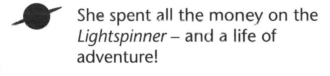 Owner of the *Lightspinner*.

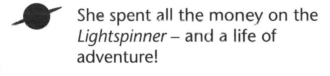 When her rich father died, Misha could have lived in luxury – but that was much too boring.

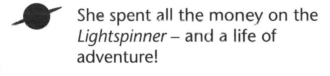 She spent all the money on the *Lightspinner* – and a life of adventure!

 Misha is the boss – but she doesn't always get her own way.

"Whenever we're in trouble, I know I've got a great team with me. The Starchasers will never let me down!"

- He may look like a cat from Earth, but he is an alien with a brilliant mind for science – and sharp teeth and claws!

- Probably the smartest cat in space. Finn and Misha don't need to tell him that – he knows!

- Suma's not always easy to get on with. Take care – he makes a dangerous enemy!

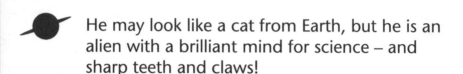

"Misha tells people I'm just a big softy. The biggest softy in the galaxy. You know what? She's wrong."

- Finn is a great guy to have around when there's trouble – and for the Starchasers, that's most of the time.

- Probably the best pilot Planet Earth has ever produced – though Misha and Suma don't tell him that, of course!

- Finn is great for getting the Starchasers out of (and sometimes in to) trouble! If only he didn't love gadgets so much …

"I was in big trouble when Misha found me in an on-line computer game. She changed my life!"

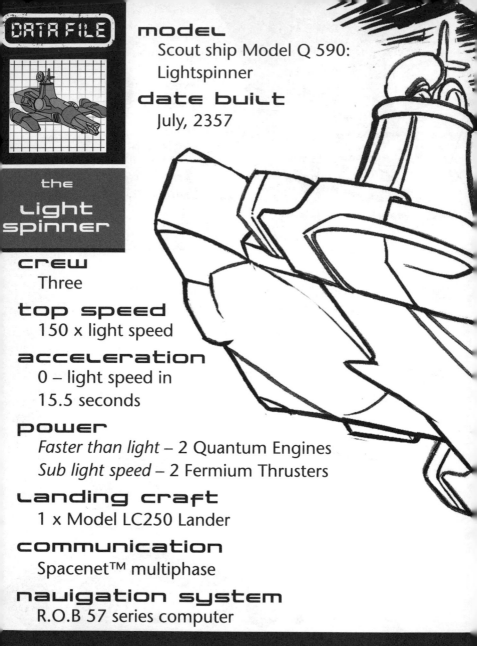

the Light spinner

model
Scout ship Model Q 590:
Lightspinner

date built
July, 2357

crew
Three

top speed
150 x light speed

acceleration
0 – light speed in
15.5 seconds

power
Faster than light – 2 Quantum Engines
Sub light speed – 2 Fermium Thrusters

landing craft
1 x Model LC250 Lander

communication
Spacenet™ multiphase

navigation system
R.O.B 57 series computer

"THE TOP-OF-THE-RANGE SOUND
SYSTEM WILL BLOW YOUR MIND!"

SPACE SOUNDS   APRIL 2357

"THE NEW Q590 – LIGHT SPEED IN 15.5 SECONDS – YOU'RE GONNA LOVE THIS BABY!"
WHAT SPACESHIP JANUARY 2357

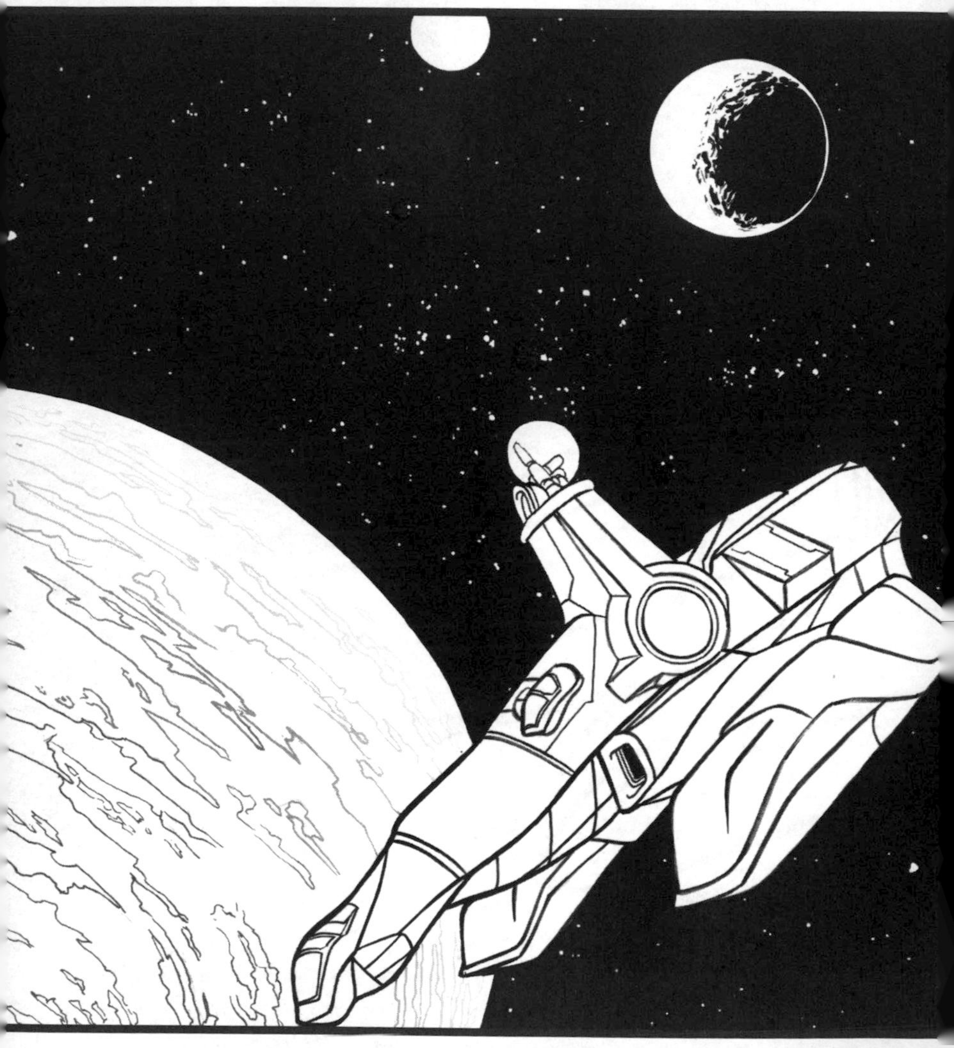

big trouble

The trouble started when the Lightspinner popped out of quantum space in the wrong place.

'Hey Finn, this isn't right!' said Misha, checking the scanner. 'You must have made a mistake when you set the navigation computer.'

Finn didn't make mistakes like that. Setting the navicom correctly was vital. Otherwise, you could end up in the middle of a sun!

'Look, Misha, here are the settings I used. They're spot on!'

Suma padded over to check.

'For once, Misha, I have to agree with Finn! There's no problem with the figures!'

Misha checked the scanner again.

'Better find out where we are, Finn.'

Finn set up Rob, the ship's computer, to do a position check. This took a while. At last the result came up on the screen.

'Lightspinner is now in Earth orbit.'

'What do you mean, Earth orbit, you stupid computer?' yelled Finn. 'We're not in orbit around any planet! And that sun over there does not look like Earth's Sun!'

Suma pushed Finn out of the way and sat down at the control desk. He started to run some checks.

'Rob's loaded with viruses,' he said. 'And they've gone deep. Finn, you haven't been bringing some of your crazy gadgets on board again … have you?'

'Oh no! I think it might be my fault,' said Misha. 'You know Rob needed an upgrade? Well, when I checked the price of the software – we just couldn't afford it!'

'So we're not running the upgrade?'

'Well, we are running *an* upgrade. I met this guy from Sirius in the spaceport on Rigel 3. He had this pirate software, really cheap … '

Finn and Suma didn't know what to say. Misha was their captain, and they both respected her. But she had made a big mistake — and it could cost them their lives!

euen bigger trouble

Misha, Finn and Suma were the Starchasers. They travelled the galaxy doing jobs that were too difficult or too dangerous for other people to take on. Work had been hard to find recently and money was tight. So Misha had taken a risk.

Misha checked the scanner again.

'At least we're inside a solar system, not hundreds of light years from anywhere. It's

not been explored before though – no
signal on the space radio! What do you
reckon, Suma? Can you sort Rob?'

'I'll have to shut down all the systems,
then go through the programming bit by bit
to clear out the virus before I can reboot it.
It's not going to be easy. As I said, it's gone
deep. Luckily, life support isn't affected.'

Suma shut Rob down. The humming
sound stopped. A silent spaceship felt really
weird.

Twenty-four space-hours later, Suma was still struggling with Rob. Progress was slow, and there was nothing that Finn or Misha could do to help.

Finn was resting in his cabin, listening to music, when suddenly – BANG!

The Lightspinner shook violently. Finn leapt up – or at least, that's what he meant to do. His feet shot out from under him, and he banged hard into the wall. He found himself floating in mid air.

He pulled himself into the main cabin. Bits and pieces of equipment were floating everywhere. Suma and Misha were hanging on to their desks.

'We've been hit!' Suma shouted. 'The artificial gravity field is out!'

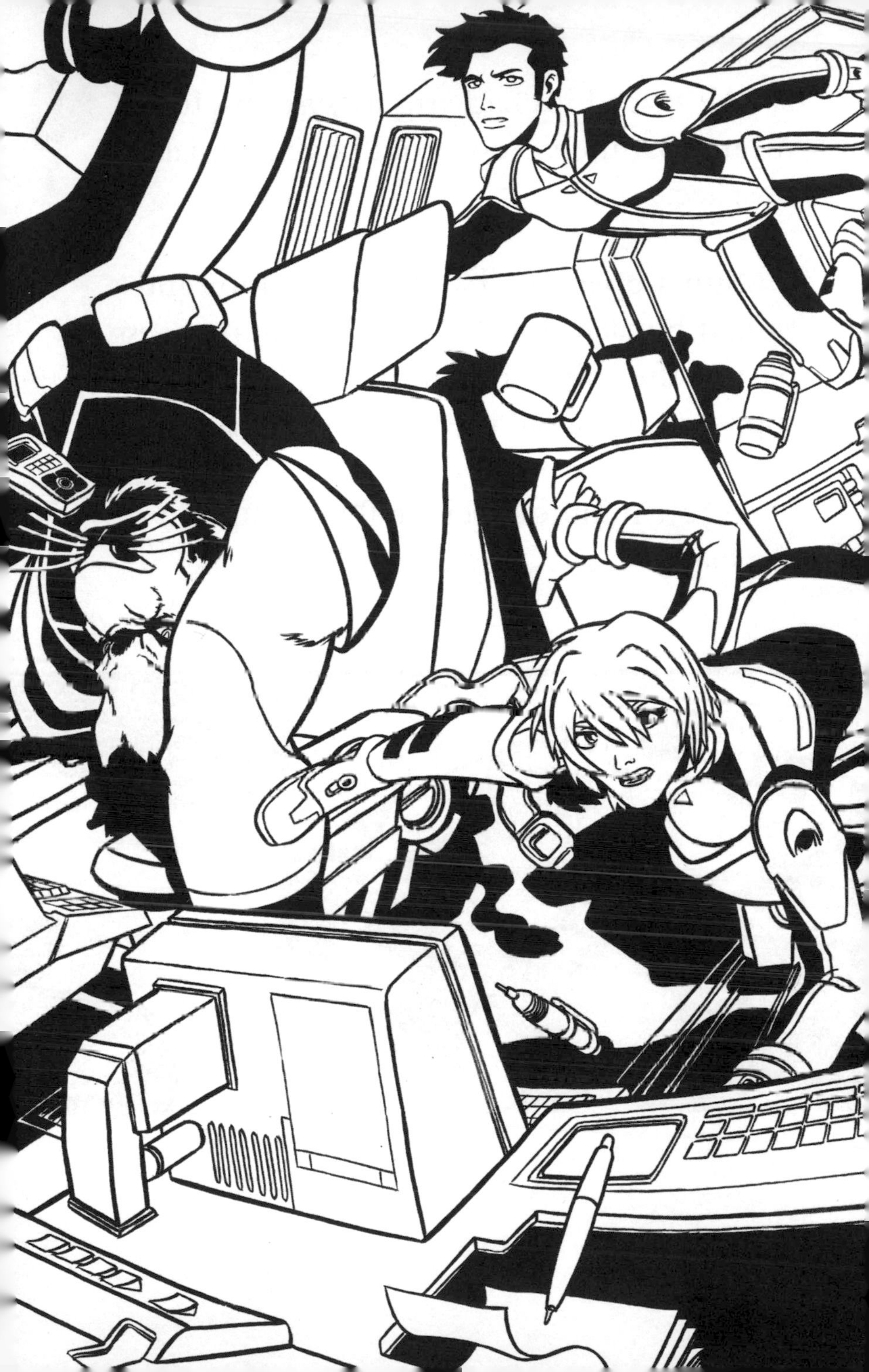

All spaceships had artgrav systems. It meant that their crews could live normally in space.

Suma opened a hatch in the floor and pulled himself down. This was the business part of the ship – quantum engine, life support, artgrav, all the things that mattered.

A few minutes later, he floated up out of the hatch.

'Now we're in big trouble, guys,' he said. 'Outside shields aren't working because the computer's down. We've been hit – just a tiny bit of space junk, but it's gone right through the artgrav.'

'Can you sort it?'

'Probably. But there's worse. The life support's been knocked out too. We've probably got just 24 hours of fresh air left!'

Landing

Suma powered up Rob just enough so that they could use the scanner.

'There's a planet in the life zone,' Misha said. 'Looks like we could breathe there. It's our only chance!'

'That's fine,' said Suma, ' – *if* we can get there! But we daren't use Rob for the landing, not with these viruses. Finn, do you think you can land without the computer?'

Finn didn't hesitate.

'It's either that or die here. Let's go for it.'

Finn was one of the best space pilots around. If he couldn't do it, no one could.

He sat down at the control desk. Getting near the planet was easy. Dropping down through the atmosphere wasn't – there were dangerous winds that could push a spaceship off course. And while you were dealing with that, you had to be looking out for a safe place to land. Usually, the computer helped with all these things. This time, Finn was on his own.

Down, down. Misha watched the scanner for possible landing places. Usually the Starchasers used a small lander for planet trips, leaving the Lightspinner in orbit. This time, they needed to get the whole ship down – and in one piece!

The atmosphere got thicker. Suma ran tests on it. Good. They would be able to breathe the air. That would give them a chance to fix the ship.

'No sign of intelligent life,' called out Misha, who was looking for things like roads and cities.

Down, down. The Lightspinner started to shake as the winds hit, but Finn was in complete control.

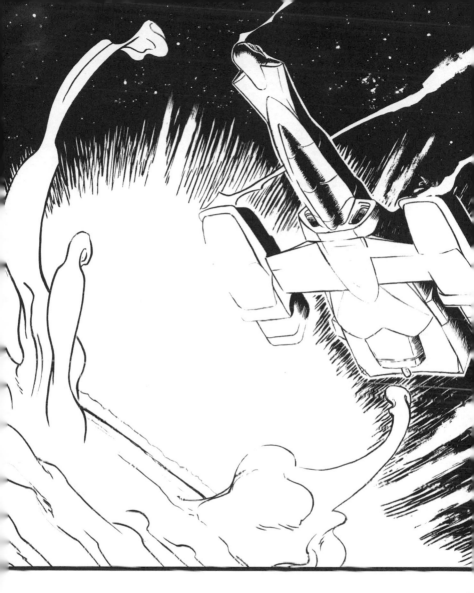

'There's an open area to the left,' Misha called out. 'Looks pretty solid. How about that?'

'Got it,' called out Finn. He changed course slightly.

'Landing legs down.'

'Engines off.'

A perfect landing. It couldn't have been better, even with Rob!

It was a relief to have gravity again, so they weren't floating around! Finn hated free fall – he always felt sick. And being sick was not good without gravity – it got everywhere!

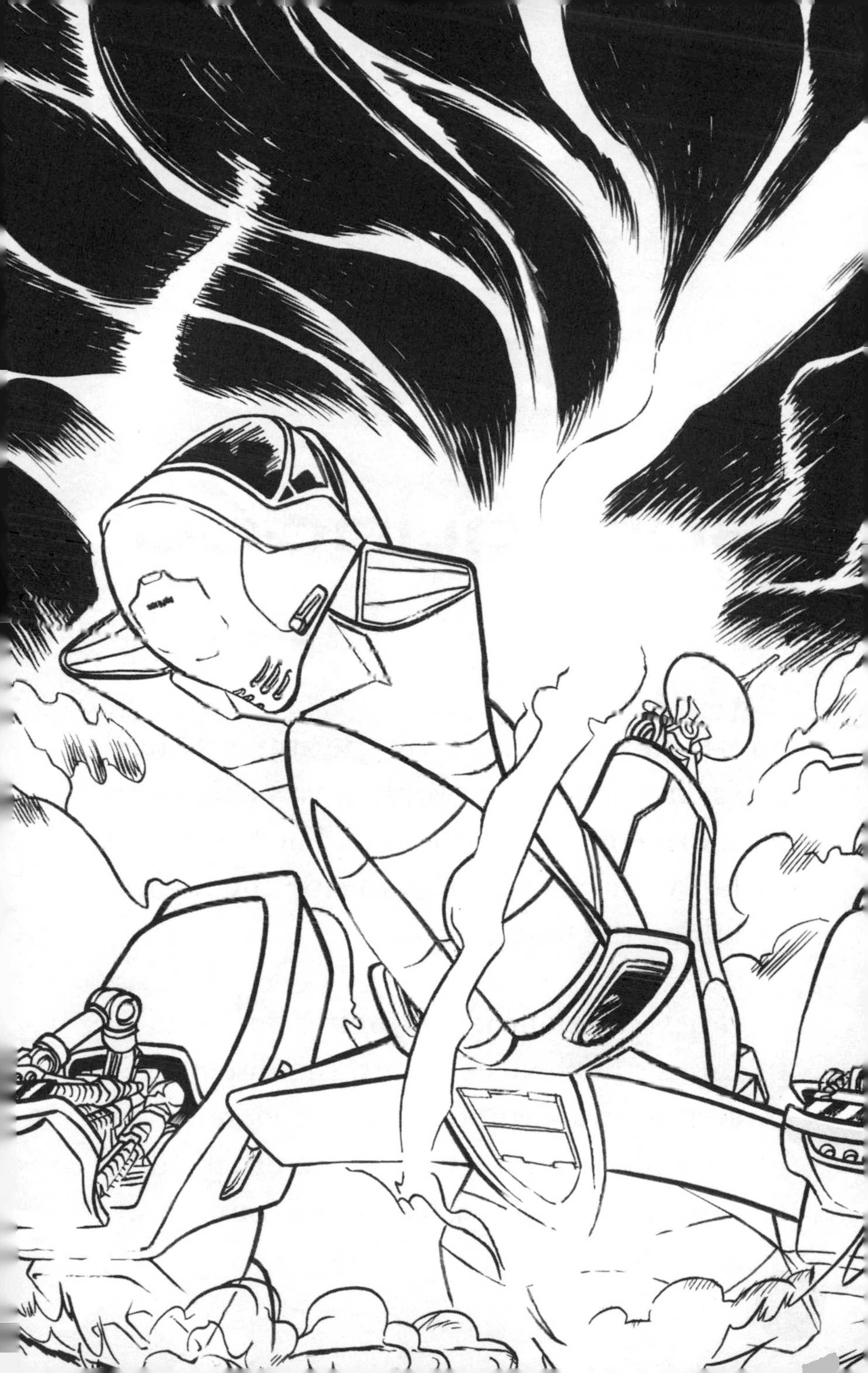

surrounded

Suma did a final check on the atmosphere. It was fine. The only problem was dangerous bugs that could make them ill. The Starchasers had to wear special filters to stop them breathing the bugs in.

They went outside. Looking one way, the grass stretched away into the distance, though it wasn't smooth – there were lumps like anthills everywhere. On the other side there were high rocks, like a cliff. Suma

guessed that the grassy place had once been
a sea. The sun was warm; very welcome
after a long time in space.

'It's a great planet!' said Finn. 'Looks like
we're the first here, wherever it is! You know
what that means, don't you?'

'What?'

'We can give it a name! How about Planet Finn?'

'Is that all you can think about?' said Suma crossly. 'We've got work to do – unless you want to live on Planet Finn for the rest of your life!'

The Starchasers checked the outside of the Lightspinner for damage. They found a tiny hole.

'That's going to be the easy bit to fix,' said Suma. 'Can you two start stripping down the life support and artgrav? I'll keep working on Rob.'

Misha was the captain, but she never minded taking orders from Science Officer Suma. She had complete trust in him.

A day on Planet Finn was a long one, thirty hours, so by the time it started to get dark the crew were feeling really tired. Suma was pleased — he was making progress at last.

The Starchasers sat outside the Lightspinner and watched the sun slowly go down.

'What was that?' said Finn suddenly.
'Over there. By that ant hill. I saw something move.'

'I can't see anything,' said Misha.

'There's definitely something there.
Look at Suma!'

Misha looked. His whiskers were
twitching, and he was staring at the ant hill.

'Can't you smell it?' Suma said at last.
'No, of course you can't – you human's
can't smell anything! There's something over
there – a mammal – and I think it's watching
us!'

Finn and Misha stood up to look. A
black, cat-like creature ran out from behind
one of the ant hills. It disappeared in the
darkness, heading for the cliff.

'Probably harmless. Looks like you, Suma!'

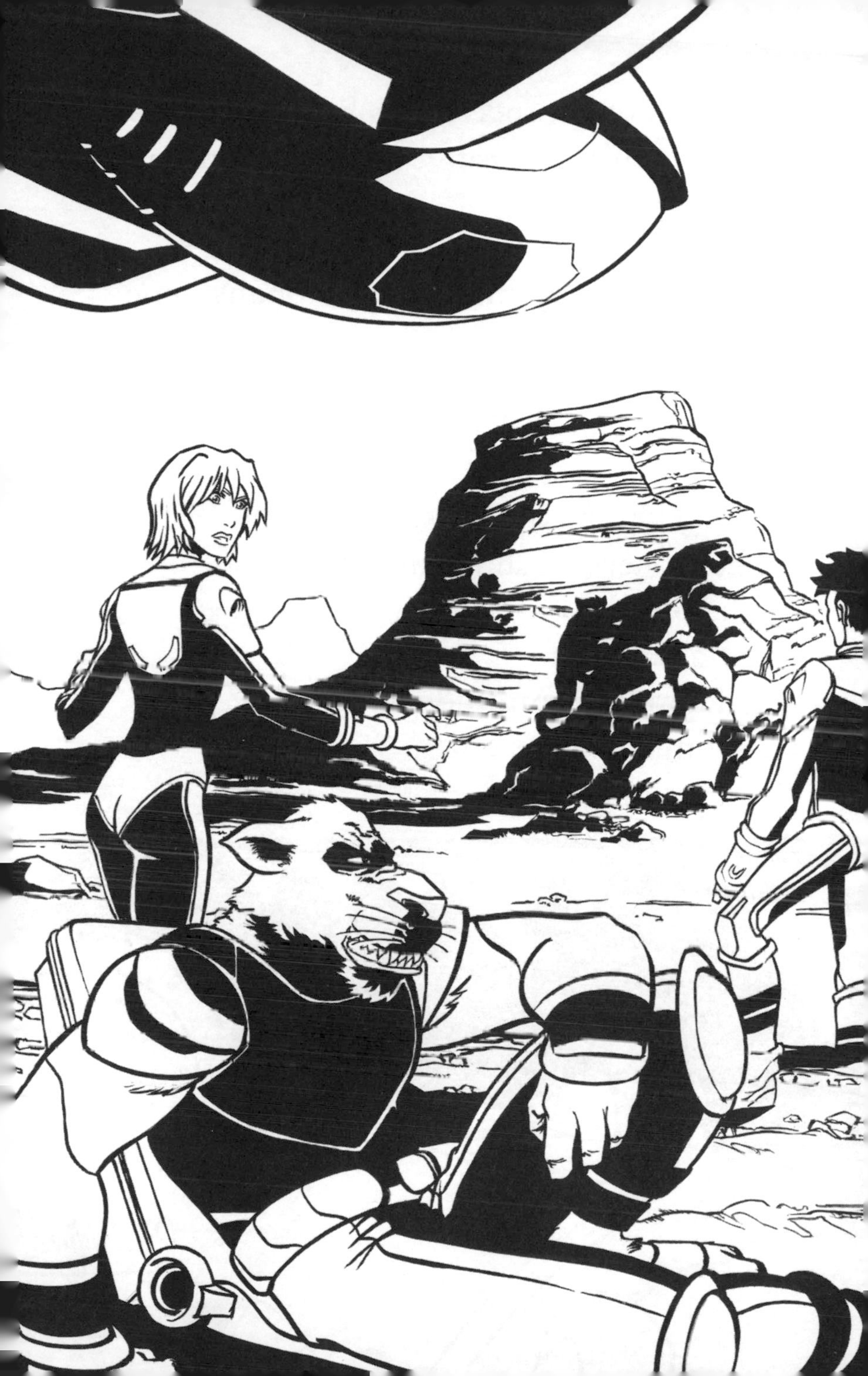

'Yes, it's a cat species. It's hard to explain, because you're not cats, but I don't think it's friendly!'

'There it is again! And it's brought some pals!'

'Let's get inside!'

Quickly, the Starchasers went into the Lightspinner and shut the airlock door. Misha switched on the outside viewer.

'There are hundreds of them! We're surrounded!'

in the cave
of the cat
people

The cat people stood in a ring around the Lightspinner. Their bodies were just dark shapes in the gloom, but their bright red eyes flashed in the darkness like danger signals.

Then one of the cats threw back its head and let out a long, sad howl. Soon all the cats were joining in.

'Misha, look at Suma!'

Suma's eyes were staring, then he too started to howl, a dreadful sound that Misha and Finn had never heard before.

'Shut the sound off, quick!'

Finn jumped to the control desk and switched off the sound and vision from outside. Suma stopped howling and shook horribly. At last he was able to speak.

'Sorry guys. It was that sound. Somehow, deep inside, I knew it.'

Sunrise came, and the team were ready for another tough day. The cats had disappeared.

'I reckon they must be nocturnal,' Misha said. 'There shouldn't be a problem during the day. I'll fix the hole outside.'

But Misha was wrong.

Suma was studying a screen full of computer code and muttering to himself. Finn was down in the engine room, trying to fix the life support system. Luckily, it wasn't too badly damaged.

The outside sound monitor was switched on, in case Misha needed anything.

There was a scream.

'Quick, Finn! Misha's in trouble!'

Suma switched on the monitor screen. There were about twenty of the cat people outside. They must have crept silently up on Misha and grabbed her before she knew what was happening. She was tied up, and the cats were dragging her off on a sort of sledge.

'Quick, Finn! Launch the jetbike! We'll never catch them on foot!'

It took a few minutes to launch the jetbike. Luckily, the cats and the sledge left a trail through the grass that Finn and Suma could follow.

'They're heading for the cliffs!'

The trail disappeared at the entrance to a cave. Finn parked the jetbike.

'Finn, keep close.'

Once in the cave, even Finn could smell the cats. The tunnel was narrow, but it soon opened out into a huge space. There was a hole in the roof that let in some daylight.

Then Finn had a shock.

'Over there, Suma! Cages! Suma, there are human beings in them!'

suma roars

There wasn't time for Suma to reply. The black cats had arrived.

They saw Finn first, and came at him menacingly. Then Suma stepped out of the shadows. At the sight of him, the cat people stood still, silent, waiting.

Suma opened his mouth and roared. The back cats stepped back. Suma stepped towards them. Straight away, all of the black

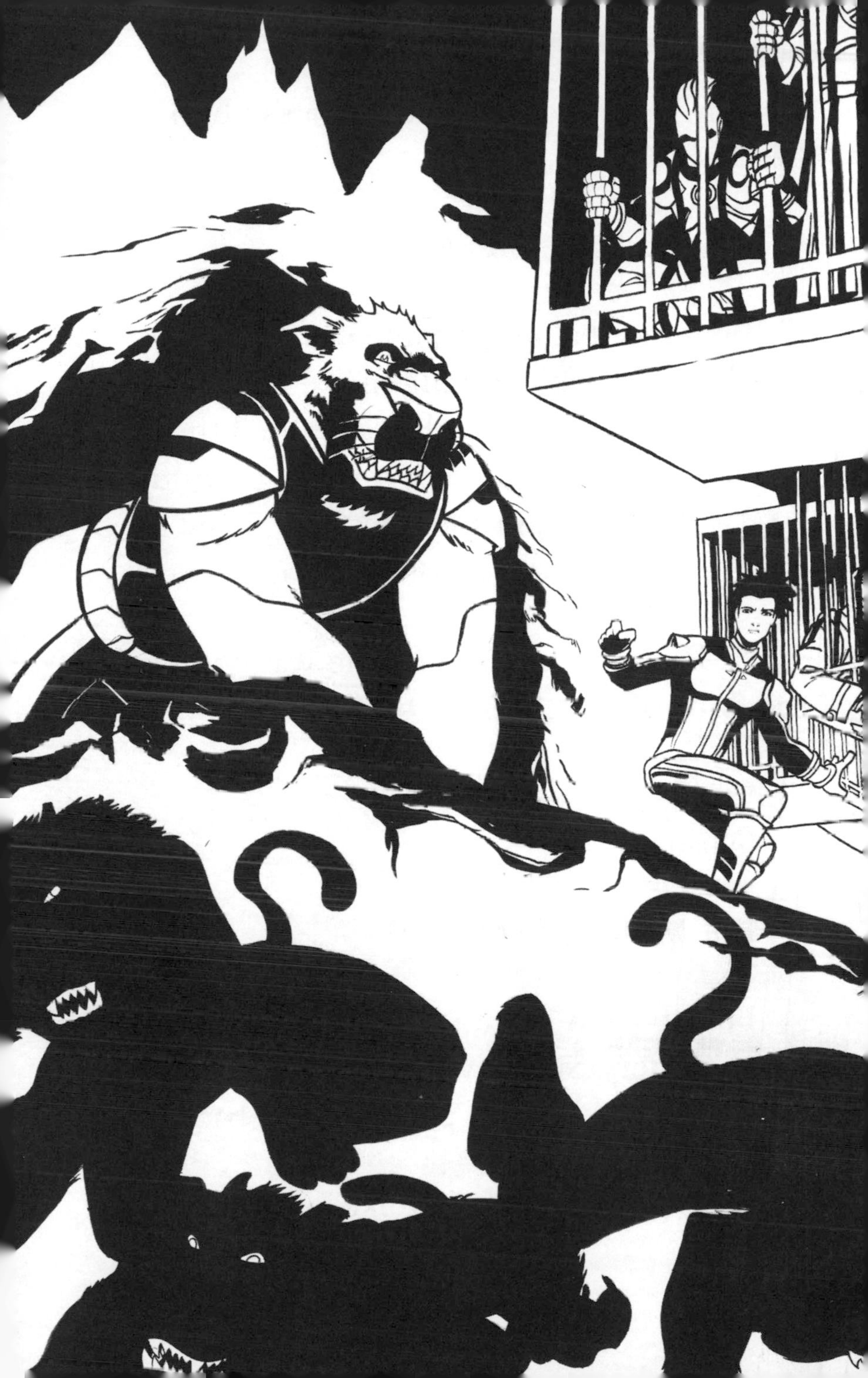

cats turned and disappeared into the back of the cave.

'Quick, Finn. Find Misha!'

Finn raced along the line of cages. Each one had a human-looking figure in it, but when Finn looked closely he realised they weren't human at all – they had big round eyes and grey, stupid-looking faces. They lay slumped in the corners of their cages.

At last he found Misha. She was lying on the floor of a cage. Finn forced open the lock.

'Misha, it's me!'

But Misha didn't move.

Finn picked her up and threw her over his shoulders. Suma was standing guard outside in case the cat people came back.

'Let's get her to the jetbike, quickly!'

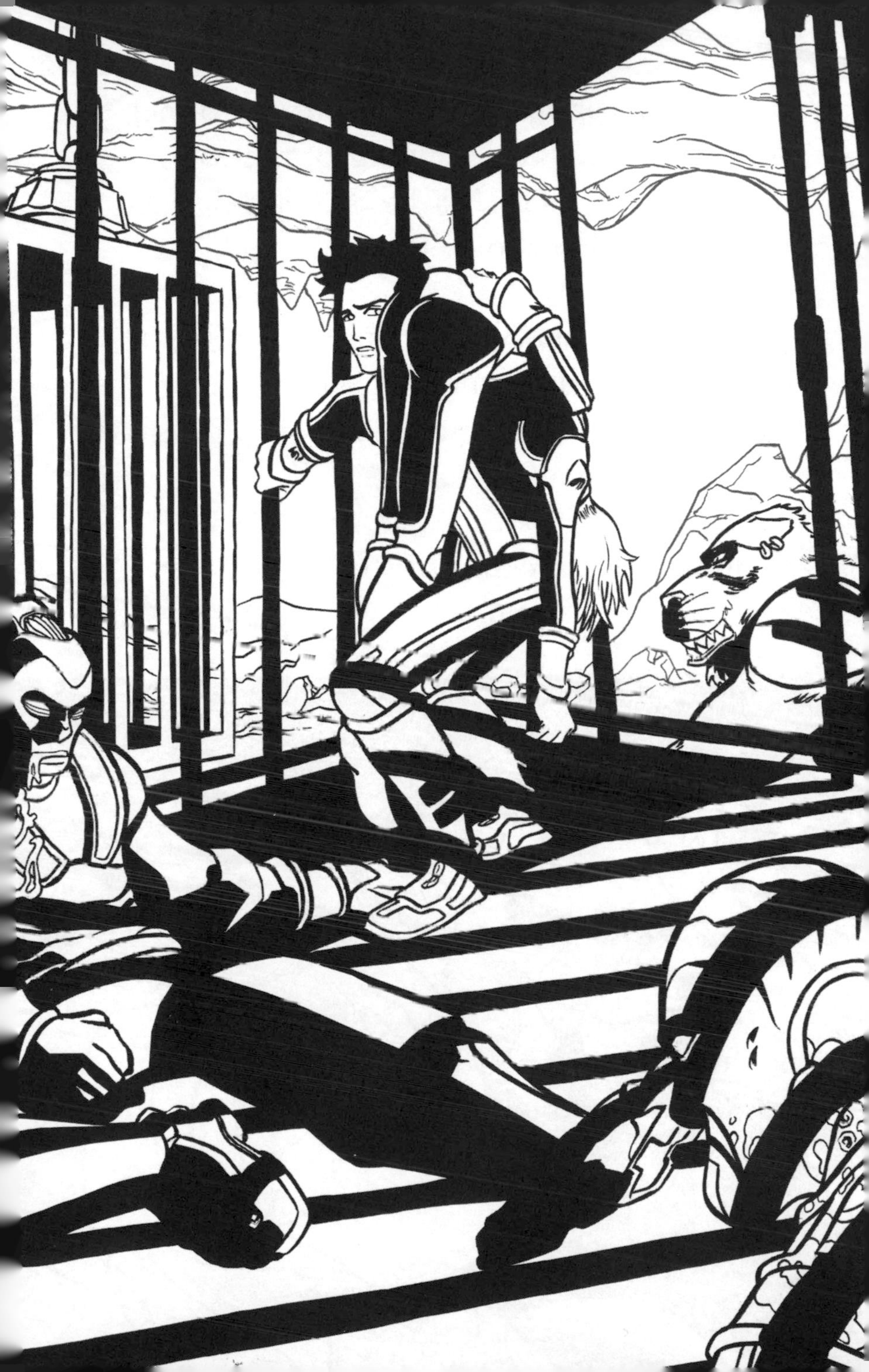

As they started down the narrow tunnel they could hear the howling of the cat people behind them. Maybe they had decided that Suma was not to be feared after all.

Misha was heavy, but Finn was strong. They dashed out of the cave. He bundled her onto the jetbike and they took off just as the cat people arrived.

Suma was checking Misha out.

'She's not dead. She looks very pale, but I think she's O.K.'

Then Suma spotted something on Misha's neck. Teeth marks.

'Finn, these aren't any sort of cat people I know. They're vampires!'

broke?

Misha had lost quite a lot of blood, but by the time they were back at the Lightspinner she was able to talk.

'It was awful! They hypnotised me with those red eyes – I couldn't move! Then I felt those teeth going in my neck!'

'These creatures are really fascinating, aren't they?' said Suma.

'Oh thanks, Suma. I'm glad you enjoyed the experience. I didn't!'

'Sorry, Misha. But the good news is that you would have been no use to them dead. My guess is that there is something missing in the diet of these creatures. They

need blood. That's why they keep those human-like creatures in cages – fast food!'

'So how come you were able to frighten them off, Suma?'

'The colour of my fur. It must have looked white and spooky in that light – those cats had black fur!'

'Brilliant! So how did you know they were going to be scared of you?'

'I didn't. It was just a lucky guess.'

'Suma, we could have been killed going in there!'

'Yes, and I thought we probably would be. But we had to rescue Misha. Anyway, I guessed it was *your* blood they wanted, not mine.'

A couple of days later, the work on the Lightspinner was done. It wasn't perfect, but it would get them home, where they could do some proper repairs. Misha called the team together.

'Guys, it was all my fault, and I'm sorry. At least now we can get home. But we've still got that software problem. We just can't afford the upgrade. I'm afraid the Starchasers are flat broke.'

Suma went into his cabin and brought

out a pouch. He emptied it on to the table. They were rocks – but rocks that shone with a beautiful blue light.

'Wherever did you get these?'

'You know those ant hills? Well, they weren't ant hills at all. I thought that the grassy place had once been an ocean. I dug around in them and found these. I guess they are the fossils of sea creatures. I've never seen anything like them. I know people that will pay big money for these – and only we know where to find them!'

'There is a problem though,' said Misha. 'Those cat people might be vampires, but they are intelligent. You know the rules about landing on planets with intelligent species.'

Suma was cross.

'Whenever I come up with a good idea ...'

'I know, I spoil it. But this lot should

fetch a good price. And – well, you never
know, the computer might just go wrong
again … '

'And by accident, we might just end up
on Planet Finn!' said Finn. 'We're going to
be rich! So where exactly was that planet?'

Suddenly Suma went very quiet.

'What's up, Suma?'

'The location of the planet! I've just
thought! We lost it when we rebooted the
computer! We'll never find it again!'